The adven

See Otto
Say
Hi!

David Milgrim

Ready-to-Read

Simon Spotlight

New York   London   Toronto   Sydney   New Delhi

This book is dedicated to the friendly

SIMON SPOTLIGHT
An imprint of Simon & Schuster Children's Publishing Division
1230 Avenue of the Americas, New York, New York 10020
This Simon Spotlight edition December 2023
Copyright © 2023 by David Milgrim
All rights reserved, including the right of reproduction
in whole or in part in any form.
SIMON SPOTLIGHT, READY-TO-READ, and colophon are registered
trademarks of Simon & Schuster, Inc.
For information about special discounts for bulk purchases, please contact
Simon & Schuster Special Sales at 1-866-506-1949
or business@simonandschuster.com.
The Simon & Schuster Speakers Bureau can bring authors to your live event.
For more information or to book an event contact the Simon & Schuster Speakers Bureau
at 1-866-248-3049 or visit our website at www.simonspeakers.com.
Manufactured in the United States of America 1123 LAK
2 4 6 8 10 9 7 5 3 1
Library of Congress Cataloging-in-Publication Data
Names: Milgrim, David, author, illustrator.
Title: See Otto say hi! / David Milgrim.
Description: New York : Spotlight, 2023. | Series: The adventures of Otto | Audience: Ages 3 to 5. |
Summary: Otto does his utmost to befriend a bird.
Identifiers: LCCN 2023007577 (print) | LCCN 2023007578 (ebook) | ISBN 9781665936187 (hardcover) |
ISBN 9781665936170 (paperback) | ISBN 9781665936194 (ebook)
Subjects: CYAC: Robots—Fiction. | Birds—Fiction. | Friendship—Fiction. | LCGFT: Picture books.
Classification: LCC PZ7.M5955 Sdf 2023 (print) | LCC PZ7.M5955 (ebook) | DDC [E]—dc23
LC record available at https://lccn.loc.gov/2023007577
LC ebook record available at https://lccn.loc.gov/2023007578

See
Tweet
come.

See Otto say hi.

See Tweet go.

See Otto go.

"Do you want ALL the chips?"

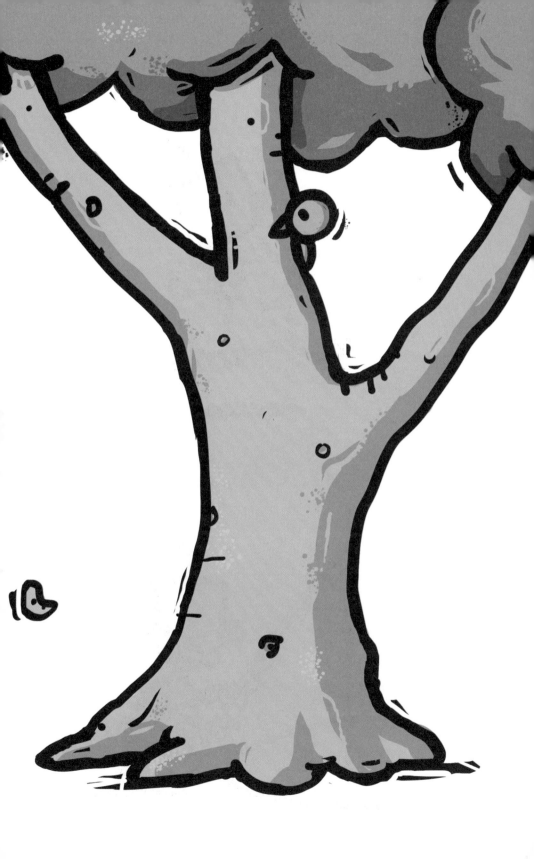

See Otto go.

Go, Otto, go.

See Otto go.

Go, go, go.

See Otto try
so hard.

See Otto try
too hard.

See Tweet go.

Go, Tweet, go!

Yum

Yum

Yum

See Otto hear Tweet!

See Otto see Tweet!

See Otto say hi.

See Tweet tweet.

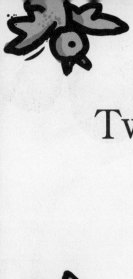

Tweet! Tweet! Tweet!

Hi, Otto!